EARLY BIRD STORIES™

Stan the Stunt Snail

Early★Reader

First American edition published in 2026 by Lerner Publishing Group, Inc.

An original concept by Cath Jones

Illustrated by Dean Gray

First published by Maverick Arts Publishing Limited

Licensed Edition
Stan the Stunt Snail

Lerner Publications Company
An imprint of Lerner Publishing Group, Inc.
241 First Avenue North
Minneapolis, MN 55401 USA

For reading levels and more information, look up this title at www.lernerbooks.com.

Main body text set in Mikado. Typeface provided by HVD Fonts.

Library of Congress Cataloging-in-Publication Data

Names: Jones, Cath, 1965–author. | Gray, Dean, illustrator.
Title: Stan the stunt snail / Cath Jones ; illustrated by Dean Gray.
Description: First American edition. | Minneapolis : Lerner Publications, 2025. | Series: Early bird readers—blue (Early bird stories) | Audience term: Children | Audience: Ages 4–8. | Audience: Grades K–1. | Summary: Stella frantically tries to help eager Stan and overconfident Fliss safely perform stunts.
Identifiers: LCCN 2024046179 (print) | LCCN 2024046180 (ebook) | ISBN 9798765670224 (library binding) | ISBN 9798765684047 (paperback) | ISBN 9798765677216 (epub)
Subjects: CYAC: Stunt performers—Fiction. | Snails—Fiction. | Animals—Fiction. | LCGFT: Animal fiction. | Readers (Publications) | Picture books.
Classification: LCC PZ7.1.J662 St 2025 (print) | LCC PZ7.1.J662 (ebook) | DDC [E]—dc23

LC record available at https://lccn.loc.gov/2024046179
LC ebook record available at https://lccn.loc.gov/2024046180

Manufactured in the United States of America
1-1011805-54066-11/21/2024

Stan the Stunt Snail

Cath Jones

Illustrated by
Dean Gray

Lerner Publications ◆ Minneapolis

"I am good at stunts," Fliss boasted.

"I am a stunt star!"

Can I be a stunt snail?

"Yes!" Fliss said.

"You can be a stunt snail."

But Stella was not sure.

What if Stan fell?

“I am good at jumping!” Fliss boasted.

“Can you help me do stunts?”

Stan said.

Fliss hopped onto a ladder.
"Hop on," she said.

Stan trusted Fliss, but Stella did not!

Stan hung on to the ladder.

At the top, Fliss did a handstand.

“Stan, wait!” Stella said.

“You need the right kit.”

She got Stan a stunt helmet
and pads for his shell.

"I am a stunt star," Fliss said.

She did a backflip off the ladder.

Fliss said, "JUMP!"

"Stan, wait!" Stella said.

"Fliss is NOT a stunt star!"

But Stan and Fliss got ready to jump!

“Stop!” Stella said.

Stan shot down the ladder like a rocket.

But a big gust of wind lifted Fliss

into the air!

“Wow-ee. This is fun!” Stan said.

But Fliss fell!

"Help!" Fliss yelled.

Stella spun a web!

Fliss and Stan landed in the web.

Thank you, Stella!

"Good job, Stella!" Fliss said.

"You are a stunt star!"

Quiz

1. What does Stan want to be?
   a) A small snail
   b) A stunt snail
   c) A super snail

2. Who does Stan ask to help him do stunts?
   a) Fliss
   b) Fran
   c) Stella

3. Who does not trust Fliss?
   a) Stan
   b) Fran
   c) Stella

4. What makes Fliss fall off the ladder?

   a) A big gust of wind

   b) Water on the ladder

   c) A web

5. What does Stella spin to save Stan and Fliss?

   a) A helmet

   b) A web

   c) A ladder

Quiz Answers: 1b, 2a, 3c, 4a, 5b

COLOR	GRL
Silver	L-P
Gold	K-L
Purple	J-K
Orange	H-J
Green	G-I
Blue	E-G
Yellow	C-E
Red	C-D
Pink	A-C

Leveled for Guided Reading

Early Bird Stories have been edited and leveled by leading educational consultants to correspond with guided reading levels. The levels are assigned by taking into account the content, language style, layout, and phonics used in each book. Visit www.lernerbooks.com for more Early Bird Readers titles!